Helen Lester

The Revenge of
the Magic Chicken

Illustrated by Lynn Munsinger

Houghton Mifflin Company
Boston 1990

For Robin and Jamie — H.L.

Books by Helen Lester and illustrated by Lynn Munsinger

The Wizard, the Fairy, and the Magic Chicken
It Wasn't My Fault
A Porcupine Named Fluffy
Pookins Gets Her Way
Tacky the Penguin
The Revenge of the Magic Chicken

Library of Congress Cataloging-in-Publication Data

Lester, Helen.
   The revenge of the Magic Chicken / Helen Lester: illustrated by
Lynn Munsinger.
     p. cm.
   Summary: When the Magic Chicken attempts revenge on his colleagues
in spellmaking, the Wizard and the Fairy, he finds his own magic
getting out of control.
   ISBN 0-395-50929-7
   [1. Magic—Fiction.]   I. Munsinger, Lynn, ill.   II. Title.
PZ7.L56285Re   1990   89-39597
[E]—dc20   CIP
                AC

Printed in the United States of America

HOR 10 9 8 7 6 5 4 3 2 1

One day the Wizard, the Fairy, and the Magic Chicken
were standing under a tree having their daily argument.
Each thought, "I am the greatest in the world."
And each was very jealous of the other two.

"*My* shoes are beautiful," announced the Wizard.
"*My* shoes are more beautiful," huffed the Fairy.
"*My* shoes are the most beautiful of all,"
squawked the Magic Chicken,
forgetting for a moment that chickens don't wear shoes.

Said the Fairy to the Wizard, "I can wave my star wand and turn you into a cow wizard."
And she did.

Said the Wizard to the Fairy, "I can wave my moon wand and turn you into a blueberry muffin."
And he did.

"You two look ridiculous,"
cackled the Magic Chicken.
He laughed

and laughed

and laughed.

"You think we look funny?
Let's see how you like being a ballerina," said the Fairy and the Wizard.
They waved their wands and . . . TA DA!
There stood a Ballerina Chicken with a pickle wand.

While his costume was stunning, the Magic Chicken wasn't much of a dancer.

He tripped and rolled beak—
over claws—over beak—
over claws—over beak—
over claws down the hill.

When he was safely out of sight of the others
he marched on, muttering,
"All they do is brag. Brag morning. Brag noon. Brag night.
If I had ears they would hurt.
I'll show them who is the greatest, I will.
I'll scare them with Pickle Power!"

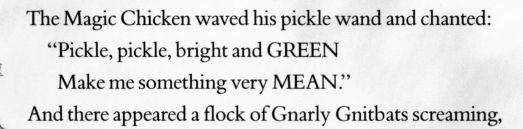

The Magic Chicken waved his pickle wand and chanted:
   "Pickle, pickle, bright and GREEN
   Make me something very MEAN."
And there appeared a flock of Gnarly Gnitbats screaming,

      "Eeeyipes! Eeeyipes!"

"There," cackled the Magic Chicken.
"That will scare those two."

Then he waved his wand and chanted the disappearing chant:
"Now make it so they can't be SEEN,
Pickle, pickle, bright and GREEN."
The flock of Gnarly Gnitbats disappeared.

Very excited, the Magic Chicken raced back, clucking, "Pickle Power, Pickle Power, Pickle Power" all the way.

He hid in the tree and could barely keep from cackling out loud.

Below, the Wizard and the Fairy
were still arguing.

The Magic Chicken waved his wand and whispered:
   "Pickle, pickle, bright and GREEN
      Make me something very MEAN."
And there on the tree appeared the flock of
Gnarly Gnitbats screaming,

   "Eeeyipes! Eeeyipes!"

The Magic Chicken was so pleased with himself,
he waved his wand and chanted again:
"Pickle, pickle, bright and GREEN
Make me something very MEAN."

And there appeared a pair of Awesome Alligators
roaring, "RrrrG, rrrrG."
"Eeeyipes! Eeeyipes!" screamed the Gnarly Gnitbats.

The Magic Chicken was having so much fun
he cackled again.

"Pickle, pickle, bright and GREEN
    Make me something very MEAN."

And there appeared an Enormous Elephant snorting,
"Harrumph! Harrumph!"
"RrrrG, rrrrG," roared the Awesome Alligators.
"Eeeyipes! Eeeyipes!" screeched the Gnarly Gnitbats.

CREAK went the tree.

The awful things were awfully heavy.
Too heavy for the tree.
It began to bend right over the heads of
the Wizard and the Fairy.
"Oh dear!" thought the Magic Chicken.
"I only wanted to scare them a little.
I didn't want to squash them."

He waved his wand as fast as he could
and chanted the disappearing chant:
"Now make it so they can't be SEEN
Pickle, pickle, bright and RED."

The Enormous Elephant kept harrumphing
and the Awesome Alligators kept rrrrGing
and the Gnarly Gnitbats kept eeeyiping.
And the tree kept bending and cracking.

The worried Magic Chicken tried again:
"Now make it so they can't be SEEN
Pickle, pickle, bright and YELLOW."
"Eeeyipes!" went the Gnarly Gnitbats.
"RrrrG," went the Awesome Alligators.
"Harrumph," went the Enormous Elephant.
CRACK went the tree.

Beneath the tree the Wizard turned to the Fairy.

"Fairy, are you making funny noises?"

"Certainly not," answered the Fairy.

"I thought it was you."

The whole tree began to shake.
The Magic Chicken waved his wand frantically
and begged once again:
"Now make it so they can't be SEEN
Pickle, pickle, bright and . . . and . . . and . . ."

Leaves flew everywhere.
Green leaves. Very green leaves.

One stuck right on the Magic Chicken's beak.

"G R E E N!" screeched the Magic Chicken.

Poof! The creatures disappeared.
The Magic Chicken fell right into the laps of the Wizard and the Fairy.

Everything was quiet. No eeeyipes! No rrrrGs. No harrumphs.
The Magic Chicken hugged the Wizard and the Fairy
and blubbered, "Thank you, thank you, thank you, thank you."
They were puzzled, but the hugs felt quite good.

The Wizard said, "Magic Chicken, you may not be
as powerful as I am—"
"—or as clever as I am," cut in the Fairy.
"But," they both agreed, "you can be friendly and nice sometimes."

Then the Fairy waved her star wand twice.
The Wizard waved his moon wand twice.
In a twinkling they were themselves again.

The Magic Chicken was so embarrassed by what had happened
that he shuffled his feet, shrugged,
and took a very small nibble of his pickle.